. . . Katie sat back on her heels and stared at the shirtless little boy. Justin held up part of his toy for Katie to see, then he began to put it on its peg.

Katie thought hard. *This is real. I can't pretend anymore that nothing is happening. This is not my imagination.* Katie planted a kiss on Justin's forehead and reached for the phone.

I Won't Let Them Hurt You

by Linda Barr

To the League Against Child Abuse, Ohio Chapter, National Committee for Prevention of Child Abuse.

Cover photo by John Strange

Published by Willowisp Press, Inc.
401 E. Wilson Bridge Road, Worthington, Ohio 43085

Printed in the United States of America

10 9 8 7 6 5

ISBN 0-87406-314-0

One

"JUSTIN Stuart! I can't believe it. You've even got spaghetti sauce in your hair!" Katie said.

Two-year-old Justin stopped splashing water out of the bathtub for a second and grinned up at Katie with a crooked smile. His big brown eyes sparkled. Water dripped off his straight blond hair, which was spotted with spaghetti sauce.

Katie shook her head at Justin and laughed. *You're so cute. How can I get mad at you?* she thought. Justin hit the water with his chubby little hands, and some of it splashed on Katie.

"Come on, Justin! We have to get you cleaned up before your mom gets home." *And I still have to clean spaghetti off the high chair and the kitchen floor,* Katie thought to herself. *It's probably on the walls, too.*

Maybe it was because Katie was an only

child that she had grown so attached to Justin in such a short time. This was her second week of baby-sitting for the Stuarts, and Katie really looked forward to watching their little boy every Tuesday and Thursday afternoon. He was so sweet. Baby-sitting him was much better than going home to an empty house, since her mother wouldn't be home from work yet anyway.

I sure don't want Mrs. Stuart to come home and find this mess, Katie thought. She wanted Mrs. Stuart to think that she was the very best baby-sitter around. This job was great. She not only adored Justin, but Katie needed the money. The Spring Dance was only two months away, and she really wanted to buy a special dress to wear.

Katie had been so excited when Scott Dennis had asked her to the dance. She and Scott had been studying together a couple times a week since last fall. He lived just two blocks away on Walnut Street, and was in three of Katie's classes at Northview High School.

Katie—and a lot of her friends—thought Scott was one of the nicest guys in their ninth-grade class. Not only did Katie think he was the best-looking, but he was quiet and kind of serious. That, Katie thought, made him special. He was different from the other boys in her class—more grown up somehow. Ever since the first time they studied together, Katie had hoped that someday Scott would ask her to go out with him. And now that he had, she wanted to look her best.

Katie tried to get Justin to lean back in the tub so she could rinse the spaghetti sauce out of his hair. She had barely accomplished that when Justin started splashing with his hands again. "Justin! You aren't making this very easy!" she groaned. Just then the phone rang.

Carefully she pulled the slippery little boy out of the tub. Then she threw a towel over him and carried the wet, wriggling child into the bedroom.

"Hello?" she said breathlessly into the phone.

"Katie!" It was Katie's best friend, Liz Humphrey. "I saw some great dresses at the mall just now!"

"Great for you or great for me?" Katie asked. Even though they had been best friends since fourth grade, Katie and Liz had totally different tastes in clothes. Katie thought Liz looked great in her wild color combinations, but they just weren't right for Katie.

Katie sat down on the edge of the Stuarts' bed and tried to keep Justin from grabbing the phone. "Me talk! Me talk!" Justin yelled.

"Dusty talk!" Justin couldn't quite say his name right yet. "Hi, Gamma!" he yelled at the phone.

"No, Justin!" Katie laughed. "It's not your grandma!"

"Oh, Katie, there was one dress that was just perfect for you!" Liz was saying. "It's long and white, kind of lacy. The skirt has a slit partway up the side with pink ruffles showing through. It's *you*, Katie!"

Katie smiled. It sounded wonderful. "How much is it?" she asked.

"Whoops—I forgot to look at the price," said Liz.

Just then, Katie felt a peculiar warmth spread down her chest. "Justin!" she groaned. He had wet all over her shirt!

"I'll call you later, Liz!" Katie blurted into the receiver.

Hurriedly Katie slammed down the phone and ran into the bathroom with Justin. She sat him on the toilet, but he looked up at her sweetly and said, "Dusty all done!"

Nice work, Dusty, Katie thought to herself. The front of her shirt was soaked. She gingerly unbuttoned it. Then she dropped it into the bathwater. Justin grinned at her from his perch on the toilet. "Please sit still a second," she begged.

Katie noticed one of Mrs. Stuart's shirts hanging on the back of the bathroom door. She put it on while she swished her own shirt around in the bathtub. *How does Mrs. Stuart keep up with Justin?* Katie wondered.

The Stuarts moved in a couple houses down from Katie and her mom only two months ago. Katie and Liz had seen Mr. Stuart drive by in his red sports car. They thought he looked like a movie star or something. And Mrs. Stuart seemed like a good match for him. She was small and pretty with thick, curly blondish brown hair that cascaded over her shoulders. Katie guessed that she was about 22, but Mr. Stuart seemed to be older. Katie's mother had told her that Mr. Stuart was the new vice president of the biggest bank in town.

Katie took Justin into his room and quickly dressed him. "Cookie?" he asked hopefully.

"Not yet," Katie answered. "First I have to dry out my shirt. Where's Mommy's clothes dryer?"

Justin just stuck his thumb in his mouth and looked up at her with his huge brown eyes. *The dryer must be in the basement,* she decided. She knew where the basement door was because Mrs. Stuart had warned her to make sure it was always closed so Justin wouldn't try going down the stairs.

9

Katie grabbed her wet shirt, squeezed most of the water out of it, and led Justin down the basement stairs one step at a time. While Katie tried to figure out how the dryer worked, Justin wandered over to a rowing machine in the corner.

"Stay over here, Justin," she called as she studied the dials on the dryer. *Thud!* Justin had tripped over a pile of clothes on the floor. He looked up at her in surprise. Then he looked down at his knee, scraped pink and raw by the rough cement floor. His little face crumpled and he started to cry.

Katie quickly sat on the cold floor and pulled him into her lap. "Oh, I bet that hurts!" she said as she hugged him. *I should have been watching him more closely,* she told herself angrily. *It's my fault he fell!*

"No cwy!" he said between sobs. "No cwy!" He shook his head and leaned against her.

"What? What did you say?" she asked, but he just kept crying. Katie rocked him awkwardly. She could feel his tears making wet patches on her borrowed shirt. "Oh, I'm sorry, Justin! I'm sorry!" she said. *How will I explain this to his mother?* she worried. She looked at Justin's knee. The scrapes were leaking little droplets of blood.

Now Mrs. Stuart probably won't trust me to

baby-sit Justin again, Katie thought. *How could I have let this happen?* Suddenly she felt like crying, too. She hugged Justin closer.

Just then she heard the garage door open. Mrs. Stuart was home!

Two

"JUSTIN? Katie?" Mrs. Stuart called.

Katie rushed up the basement stairs carrying the sobbing Justin. "He tripped and fell!" she blurted out when she saw his mother. "I'm sorry, Mrs. Stuart! I think it's my fault!"

Justin looked up at his mother and stopped crying.

"Well, let's take a look at you, Justin!" Mrs. Stuart took him from Katie. She sat him on the kitchen table so she could see his knee.

Justin hiccupped. "No cwy, Mommy! No cwy!"

"That's right, Justin. Big boys don't cry," Mrs. Stuart agreed. She helped him down and turned to Katie. "Don't worry about this, Katie. Justin falls all the time." She shook her head. "I guess he'll never be an athlete like his father."

Katie smiled a little and nodded.

"Katie, that shirt . . . ?" Mrs. Stuart asked.

Katie glanced down. She was still wearing Mrs. Stuart's shirt! "Oh, I can explain!" Katie said nervously. "Mine got wet and I was going to dry it and—" Katie gestured toward the basement door.

"Why don't you just wear that shirt home today?" Mrs. Stuart interrupted. "I'll take your shirt out of the dryer for you when it's finished."

"Uh, thanks, Mrs. Stuart. I'll bring yours back on Thursday."

"Anne! Please call me Anne!" She smiled. "I feel like someone's grandmother when you call me Mrs. Stuart!"

"Gamma?" Justin asked. He looked around the kitchen.

They both laughed. Then Katie saw Anne eyeing the spaghetti that still hung from the tray of the high chair. "I'll clean that up right now," Katie said quickly. She grabbed the sponge out of the sink.

"Oh, I'll take care of it." Anne took the sponge from Katie. "I'm used to it. I just hope Justin learns to eat with better manners pretty soon."

"Well, uh, thanks! I guess I'd better get home," Katie mumbled. "I need to study for a history test tomorrow."

"A history test," Anne repeated. "That seems like only yesterday." Anne looked lost in thought for a second. "I'll bet you have a boyfriend, too, right?" She smiled.

Katie felt herself blush. "Well, not a real boyfriend." *Not yet anyway,* she told herself. "But a boy I study with did ask me to the Spring Dance."

"Do you have a dress yet?" Anne asked. "Justin, stay away!" she called sharply.

Justin had wandered into the living room. He was reaching out to touch a delicate crystal fawn standing with its crystal mother and father on a table by the couch. Katie had noticed the deer family the first time she baby-sat and worried that Justin might try to play with it. She even considered putting the deer up on the mantel, where he couldn't reach them.

At the sound of his mother's voice, Justin quickly put both of his hands behind his back and held them tightly together. He looked at her with worried eyes. "Dusty good boy," he said.

Anne nodded at Justin, her lips pushed together in a thin line. Then she turned to Katie and smiled. "Tell me about your dress for the dance."

"I don't have one yet," Katie admitted, "but I'm saving my money to buy one."

"I'd like to see it when you get it," Anne said. "I used to love those dances." Anne turned and stared out the kitchen window. "I wish they had them for married people."

Anne looked so sad that Katie felt a little embarrassed. "Well, see you Thursday!" she said quickly. "Bye, Justin!"

"Bye-bye!" Justin waved his chubby hand at her.

"Bye, Katie," Anne said. "Thanks for your help!"

When Katie got home, she made dinner so it would be ready when her mom got home from her job at the insurance company. As they passed the salad and casserole to each other, Katie told her mom about the dress Liz had seen at the mall.

Mrs. Weber listened quietly. "Well, Katie, it sounds nice. Do you know how much it costs?" she finally asked.

Katie looked at her plate. "I'm not sure yet," she said softly.

Her mother put her fork down. She had lines under her eyes. Katie thought she looked even more tired than usual. "Well, we'll try to get out to the mall sometime. You may not be able to get it if it costs too much, honey."

"Mom, I told you I'll pay for it," Katie insisted. "Mrs. Stuart gives me $10 a week. I already have $30 saved from my other baby-sitting. The dance is still two months away. I have it all figured out! You'll see!"

Her mother slowly nodded, but Katie could tell she wasn't convinced. "How did it go today, anyway?" Mrs. Weber asked.

Katie decided not to worry her mother. She knew her mom already had plenty to think about. Mrs. Weber had just been promoted and had to learn a whole new job, including how to use a computer. She worked hard, and lately spent her evenings reading computer manuals.

"Oh, everything went great! Justin is one of the cutest kids I've ever watched." Katie poured some dressing on her salad to avoid looking at her mother.

No point in telling Mom anyway, she thought. *Nothing she could do would take away Justin's scraped knee or the spaghetti on the high chair. I just hope that the Stuarts let me keep that job!*

After dinner, Scott came over to study for their history test the next day. As they spread their study sheets and books out on the kitchen table, he asked, "So who did Liz decide to go to the big dance with?"

Two boys had asked Liz to the dance—Kenny and Mike. Mike was a football player with curly, black hair. He lived near Liz and walked her to school every day. Kenny was tall and blond. Katie thought he was so funny that he should be on television.

Katie grinned and shook her head. "Liz can't make up her mind," she told Scott. "In fact, I don't think she's even decided yet what color her hair will be for the dance!"

Scott laughed. Just last week Liz had been sent home from school because she had shown up with a green ponytail. Apparently, her homeroom teacher didn't like Liz's hair green.

"By the way, we have a new little girl at our house," Scott said. "Do you want to come over and see her later?"

Mr. and Mrs. Dennis had been foster parents for many years. Since Katie had known Scott, his parents had taken care of two children, each for a couple of months. One was a baby who was waiting for new parents to adopt her, and the other was an eight-year-old whose mother was in the hospital.

"This little girl's name is Laura and she's three and a half," Scott told Katie. "She's a pretty special girl. You'll like her when you get to know her."

What does he mean by that? Katie wondered.

Three

"SHE'S really cute!" Katie said. Laura was standing next to the couch in Scott's living room, looking up at them with big, blue eyes. Soft brown curls circled her freckled face. She was wearing a shirt with a big kitty on the front and matching pink corduroy pants.

"Hi, Laura!" Katie said softly. She smiled and knelt down in front of the little girl. Suddenly Laura started screaming. Katie was so surprised she nearly fell over backward.

Then Laura grabbed a handful of her own hair and pulled. Scott awkwardly caught her wrist. He tried to get her to let go, but she held on tightly and kept screaming. It was a strange sort of scream that Katie had never heard from a child before.

"It's all right, Laura," Scott said. Katie knew he was trying to soothe the little girl, but she could hear panic in his voice.

Mrs. Dennis rushed in and hugged Laura, pinning the little girl's arms to her sides. She pulled Laura onto her lap, and the two of them sat on the floor for several minutes while Mrs. Dennis rocked the child and talked to her softly. Finally Laura stopped screaming.

Katie had backed several steps away. Now she noticed that Laura's hair was very thin in places. Katie could see her scalp easily.

Mrs. Dennis looked up at Katie. "Laura still doesn't know us very well," she explained. "She'll be better when she's used to being here, right, Laura?" Scott's mother hugged the child and kissed her freckled nose. Laura just stared blankly at her.

"Uh, I guess I'd better be going," Katie mumbled. "It's getting late."

"I'll walk you home," Scott offered. Mrs. Dennis smiled and kept rubbing Laura's back.

As Katie and Scott walked together, the little girl's screams echoed in Katie's head. "What's wrong with Laura?" she asked. "I never saw anyone act that way before."

"My mom says Laura was abused when she was a baby," Scott answered quietly.

"You mean, someone beat her up?" Katie asked in horror.

"Not exactly," Scott told her. "When Laura

19

was about a year and a half old, her father lost his job and couldn't find another one. He stayed home with Laura while his wife worked. Laura cried a lot—I don't know why. I guess the crying really bothered her father. When she wouldn't stop crying, he shook her, like this."

Scott put his hands on Katie's shoulders and shook her gently a couple of times.

"Then how did she get abused?" Katie asked, confused.

"That's what did it," Scott explained. "I didn't understand either until my mother explained it. When you shake a baby, the brain bounces against the skull. The shaking and bouncing broke tiny blood vessels inside Laura's brain. For a while, though, no one knew anything was wrong."

"Did her father just shake her once?" Katie never knew that shaking could hurt a baby.

"No one knows for sure," Scott continued, "but he probably did it a lot, I guess. Anyway, one night Laura had convulsions. Her parents rushed her to the hospital. The doctors there guessed what had happened, but by then the broken blood vessels had made Laura's brain swell up inside her skull."

"How awful!" Katie wasn't sure she wanted to hear any more.

"Mom told me Laura spent about two weeks in the hospital. The doctors were able to save her life, but sometimes kids die from being shaken."

"I'll bet her father felt terrible!" Katie said.

"Not really," Scott told her.

Katie stopped and stared at him. "He didn't? He didn't care?" Katie felt hot tears rush to her eyes. She was glad it was getting dark so Scott couldn't see them.

"Laura's father didn't believe his shaking had hurt her. The parents just wanted to take Laura home and get away from the doctors and the hospital."

"Did the doctors let them do that?" Katie asked.

"No," Scott told her. "They called the children's social services agency, the same people who send foster kids to my parents. Their caseworkers talked to Laura's parents. They decided her life would be in danger if she stayed with them so they took Laura away and put her in foster care. Now they're looking for new parents for her."

Scott and Katie were standing on the sidewalk in front of her house. Scott looked up at the streetlight for a minute. Katie waited for him to go on, although the story made her heart ache.

"Now Laura can't talk anymore," he said. "She hasn't smiled since we've had her. When she gets scared or upset, she pulls her hair out. Sometimes she tries to bite herself."

"But she'll get better, right?" Katie asked.

Scott shook his head. "The doctors told my mom that now Laura is permanently brain-damaged from the shaking. Mom has to take her in for therapy three times a week. Now her own parents don't want her. Our house is her third foster home in a year because she is so hard to take care of."

Later that night, Katie lay awake thinking of Laura. *What kind of monster could hurt a baby?*

Four

WHEN Katie got to the Stuarts' house on Thursday, Anne was waiting for her at the door, car keys in hand.

"Am I late?" Katie asked.

Anne smiled, but Katie thought that the woman's eyes still looked angry. "No," Anne answered. "I just need to get out. . . ." She stopped and glanced down at Justin, who had run up and hugged Katie's knees. "I mean, I have a lot to do this afternoon."

Anne picked up her purse. "I left Justin's dinner in a bowl in the refrigerator. Warm it up in the microwave and make sure he eats it all." Anne looked at her son sternly. He glanced up at her with wide eyes. Then he hid his face against Katie's jeans.

"Oh, we'll get along fine," Katie said. She hoped Justin wasn't having spaghetti again. "Is there a number where I can call you?"

Anne shook her head. "I'll be shopping. You could call my husband at work if you need to." Katie knew Mr. Stuart's number was on a list beside both phones. "Don't call him unless there's really an emergency, though, okay?"

Anne left quickly, and Katie took Justin out to play in the backyard sandbox. It was full of toy trucks. "Let's make a road with this bulldozer," she suggested, but Justin just grinned at her and threw a shovelful of sand in the air.

"Don't!" Katie said. "You'll get—"

"Ow! Ow!" he yelled as he reached up to rub the sand out of his eyes. Katie caught his hands and pulled him onto her lap. Big tears ran down his cheeks, but he held still as she looked closely at his eye.

"I think your tears already took care of that bad sand," Katie told him.

"No cwy! No cwy!" Justin insisted as more tears fell.

This time Katie understood. "It's okay to cry when something hurts," Katie told Justin. "I cry sometimes, too."

"No! No!" Justin almost shouted. "Big boy no cwy! Daddy 'pank!"

"Shhhh," she said, hugging him tightly. "Come on, Justin." Katie stood him up and brushed the sand off. "You must be hungry."

But Justin wouldn't eat. Katie had carefully heated his bowl of stew to just the right temperature, the way Anne had showed her the first day she baby-sat. Then Katie handed him his little spoon with the bunny on the handle, but he shook his head and let the spoon fall out of his hand.

"What's wrong, honey?" she asked.

He just stared at her with his big brown eyes.

"Look, this is really good!" Katie took his spoon and pretended to eat a bite. Then noisily she licked her lips. "Mmmmmm! Good!"

She could see he wasn't fooled, but he did smile a little.

Katie's stomach growled. *Well,* she told herself, *I am hungry, even if you aren't.* She found another spoon in the drawer. This time she didn't pretend.

"Mmmm, this is good!" Katie was about to eat another bite, just to show Justin it was safe to eat, when he stuck his little spoon in the stew and put a tiny bite in his mouth.

Katie smiled. *I guess I'm pretty good at handling kids,* Katie thought. Then Justin winced. He opened his mouth and let the stew fall out. It dribbled down his chin onto his striped shirt. Fresh tears sparkled in his eyes.

"What . . . what's wrong?" she asked softly.

She wiped his chin with a napkin to keep more of the stew from landing on his shirt.

"Hurt," he whimpered. A tear slid down his cheek.

"What hurts? Show me," Katie told him, trying to stay calm.

Justin opened his mouth. Katie saw red marks on his top gums, alongside his little teeth. She gently pulled his lower lip down a little. There were more red marks on his lower gum.

"What happened? Did you fall down again?" she asked. Justin closed his mouth tight and stared at his hands in his lap.

Poor kid! Katie thought to herself. *That must really hurt. He must have fallen with a toy or something in his mouth. I wonder if Anne knows about this?*

His mother wanted him to eat his whole dinner, Katie remembered. *She'll understand when she finds out about his sore mouth, won't she?*

"How about some milk, Justin? That won't hurt your mouth."

Katie had already poured milk into Justin's plastic cup with the drinking spout on it. He reached for it and drank most of it down. Katie looked at the bowl of stew. Her stomach growled so loudly she almost didn't hear a car pull into the driveway.

Minutes later, Anne came in the back door, looking much more cheerful than when she left. She was carrying a bag from Katie's favorite department store—the one where all she could afford to do was look. "How did it go today?" Anne asked.

"Uh, well, fine," Katie answered. Then she saw Anne frowning at the full bowl of stew. "Uh, did you . . . did you know Justin's mouth is sore?" Katie asked. "He must have fallen or something. But not while I was here!" she added quickly.

At first Anne said nothing. She turned and put her bag on the kitchen counter. "I guess Justin did fall at the park this morning," she finally said without turning around. "I think he tripped over something in the grass."

Anne faced Katie. "He'll be fine, though," she said in a determined voice. She grabbed his bowl, walked to the sink, and quickly scraped the stew into the garbage disposal. "He really should have eaten his dinner. His father wants him to learn to eat everything on his plate."

On the short walk home, Katie wondered what she would do if she were a parent. *I would have given Justin ice cream for dinner if his mouth hurt,* she thought. *Of course, I would*

27

have eaten some too, just to keep him company!

When she got up to her bedroom, she added the $10 Anne had given her for the week to the $30 she had already saved. $40! *Maybe Mom will take me to the mall tonight,* she thought. *I've got to see that dress Liz told me about. If it's as pretty as she said, maybe I can put it on layaway until I earn the rest of the money. I hope this dress is what I want. I hope it shows Scott that I'm more than just a good friend and study partner!*

Five

THE next day at school, Katie waited and waited for Liz at their usual table in the cafeteria. *Just when I need to talk to her,* Katie fumed.

Finally she saw her friend pushing through the crowd. There was a strange jingling sound as Liz walked toward her.

"This is one of my very best ideas!" Liz announced as she slid onto the seat beside Katie. "Here! I saved one for you!"

Liz handed Katie a brownie. It looked as if someone had stuck an elbow in it. Then Liz started pulling change out of her pockets and dumping it on the table.

"Uh, Liz—" Katie began.

"I baked brownies last night," Liz interrupted. "Look at all this money! I sold them to kids for a quarter apiece. Help me count this! One or two more days of baking brownies and

I'll have all the money I need to buy my dress! Maybe I should make cupcakes tonight. What do you think?"

Liz had told Katie at lunch on Wednesday about the dress she wanted to buy for the dance. Her parents had promised to give her enough money for a dress. But if Liz wanted one that cost more than what they gave her—and she did—she had to make up the difference.

"I found my dress in the same store as yours," Liz had explained on Wednesday. "It's shocking pink and strapless! Well, actually, it has straps, but you can take them off. It looks great on me!"

Now Katie watched Liz sort out her quarters, nickels, and dimes. Katie smiled and shook her head. "Well, I have to admit this sure looks easier than baby-sitting!"

"How's that going, anyway?" Liz asked.

"Okay," Katie said. "Justin really keeps me busy, but he's so cute, I don't mind." Katie thought of the red marks she had seen in his mouth the day before. "He sure gets hurt a lot."

Liz was busy stacking quarters into piles of four. "Well, you know kids, especially boys!"

Katie nodded in agreement. "I guess you're right. But it just seems like he gets hurt more than most little kids I know."

"Well, Katie, I'm not exactly an expert when it comes to baby-sitting. Not after what happened with the Hunters last week," Liz said.

Katie laughed, remembering Liz's disastrous last baby-sitting job. It had all started when the Hunters' cat had come to the front door with a chipmunk in its mouth. When Liz opened the door, the cat came into the house and dropped the chipmunk. The little animal immediately ran under the living room couch. Liz and the two Hunter kids had spent the whole evening chasing the little chipmunk, which ran under one piece of furniture after another. The cat had tried to catch the chipmunk, too, until Liz had shut the cat in the bathroom.

When Mrs. Hunter came home, most of the furniture was out of place and the cat was yowling in the bathroom. The kids had missed dinner, their baths, and their bedtimes. Mrs. Hunter didn't mind . . . in fact, she thought the whole thing was funny. But Liz decided she wouldn't baby-sit again for a *long*, long time.

Just then someone with a deep voice said, "Excuse me."

"I'm out of brownies. I'll have more tomorrow," Liz said without glancing up.

"No, you won't," the voice boomed. Both

girls quickly looked up to see Vice Principal Cramer standing beside their table. "Selling food in the school cafeteria without permission is against the rules here," he said sternly. "You, Miss Humphrey, should know that."

Katie breathed a huge sigh of relief after Mr. Cramer walked away. Her heart was still racing, though.

Liz plopped her head on her hand and sighed. "Now how am I going to earn the rest of the money I need for the dress?"

Katie thought for a minute. "How about getting a paper route, Liz? A girl in my homeroom has one. She says she makes a lot of money with it."

"I thought of that," Liz told her friend, "but then I remembered you have to deliver papers even on rainy days. I can't go outside when it rains. You know how frizzy my hair gets!" She tossed her ponytail, which was blondish brown today.

"There's got to be another way," Liz said as she dumped her lunch out on the table. She gave Katie a strange look. "How much money can I get for a quart of my blood, do you think?"

"Blood? Yuck! You really are desperate!" Katie told her. "Anyway, I think you have to be at least 16 or 18 to do that."

"Whew! That's good!" Liz said. "I don't think I'm brave enough for that!"

Katie grinned. Then she frowned. "By the way, I found that dress you told me about at the mall last night."

Liz smiled as she started pushing the change off the table into her empty lunch bag. "Great! What do you think? Nice, huh? Don't you think it looks sophisticated?"

Katie sighed. "It's beautiful. It's perfect." Katie rested her chin in her hand and stared at the table.

Liz looked up. "Well, you sure don't seem thrilled," she commented. "What's wrong, Katie?"

"My mom wouldn't let me put the dress on layaway," Katie blurted out. "She thinks it costs too much!" Katie put down her sandwich. Suddenly she didn't feel like eating her lunch, not even the squashed brownie.

"Oh, Liz! I fell in love with it! Now someone else is going to buy it before I do!" Katie stuffed her sandwich and the brownie into her lunch bag.

Liz nodded. "I guess we both have to make the rest of the money we need, quick!"

Katie sighed. "At least your parents are giving you most of your money. If my dad sent the money he was supposed to, my mom might pay for part of my dress, too." She stared at her beat-up sneakers. "One thing I know for sure—I'm not going to be poor all my life! My marriage isn't going to turn out like my mom's!"

Katie's parents had divorced when she was barely two years old. The only thing she could remember about her dad was the wire frames of the glasses he wore. Sometimes she wished her mother hadn't thrown out all his pictures.

Her father was supposed to send money each month to help her mom out, but some months the check was late. Twice last year it didn't come at all.

Later that night, Scott walked over to Katie's house so they could study for an English test the next day. After about an hour of trying to understand participles, though, Katie's mind started to wander.

"How's Laura doing?" she asked.

"She's a *lot* better now," Scott said. "She hasn't pulled her hair in a week. In fact, the agency has a family that wants to adopt Laura," he told Katie. "If it works out, she might go live with them in about two weeks."

"Great!" Katie said. Then she shook her head. "I still can't believe her parents don't want her. If I had a little girl, I'd love her no matter what."

Of course, Katie told herself, *if I were Laura's mother, I never would have let her get hurt in the first place. When I get older,* she decided, *my marriage isn't going to be like my mother's or like Laura's parents'. It's going to be just like Anne Stuart's! She has a nice husband, a cute little boy, and plenty of money. I think her life must be almost perfect.*

Six

THE following Tuesday, as Katie hurried up the Stuarts' front sidewalk and reached out to ring their doorbell, she heard Anne yelling. "Stop crying! It's a good thing your father isn't here to see you act this way!"

Uh-oh, Katie thought. *Maybe I should wait a while before I go in. No,* she decided, *I'll be late if I do that.* Katie pushed the doorbell. For a few minutes nothing happened.

When Anne finally opened the door, Katie saw what had taken her so long. Justin had wrapped himself around Anne's leg, and she was trying to pull him off. Her peach-colored linen pants had damp circles on them from his tears. Justin's face was red and blotchy as he struggled to hold on.

"No go! No go, Mommy! Dusty good boy!" Justin yelled up at her between hiccups.

"I'll be back later," Anne told Katie. She

jerked away from her son, grabbed her jacket off a nearby chair, and headed for the door to the garage.

Katie stood in the front doorway for a minute, not sure what to do. Justin had never seemed to mind his mother leaving before.

"Mommy! No go! Dusty be good!" Katie could hear panic in Justin's voice. "Mommy!" he yelled as he ran after his mother. Katie hurried to stop him.

She caught him just before the door to the garage slammed shut behind his mother. Suddenly Justin stopped struggling to get away from Katie and went limp in her arms. He looked up at her. "No go? Tatie no go?" he asked in a shaky little voice.

"No, honey, I won't go," she promised. Katie wondered why he was making such a fuss about his mother leaving. She scooped him up and carried him to the soft beige couch in the Stuarts' living room. Justin snuggled against her and sat still for longer than she had thought possible. Twice she checked to see if he had fallen asleep. He just sat sucking his thumb.

As Katie cuddled him, she glanced at the end table nearest them. The crystal fawn was missing. Only the buck and the doe stood there on their fragile legs. Maybe Anne had just put the fawn someplace higher so Justin wouldn't touch it, Katie hoped.

"Hey, Justin," Katie called softly. Her legs were falling asleep. "Let's go to the park, okay?"

Justin shook his head. Justin also was not interested in playing in his sandbox. Finally, Katie had to go to the bathroom. She had to promise to come right out before Justin would let go of her.

The two watched *Sesame Street* for an hour. Then Katie realized she hadn't asked Anne what Justin should eat for dinner. She eased him off her lap and went into the kitchen. He followed her so closely she had to be careful not to step on him.

In the refrigerator Katie found a plate with a cooked hamburger patty, corn, and beets on it, all ready for Justin, it seemed. "Well, are you hungry?" she asked.

Justin seemed to think for a minute. Then he smiled and nodded. "Dusty good boy. Eat all up!" *At least he's happier now,* Katie told herself. *I wonder why he made such a fuss today.*

Katie helped Justin into his high chair while his dinner heated in the microwave. He seemed eager to eat, but Katie hadn't forgotten what had happened last Thursday. "Does your mouth still hurt?" she asked.

"No." He smiled again and shook his head. "No hurt."

Justin wolfed down his dinner, eating with both hands and occasionally his spoon. He even gobbled up the beets.

"Look, Tatie! Good boy!" Justin said when he finished. All smiles, he picked up his empty plate to show her. Katie smiled back. But then Justin vomited his whole dinner all over his clothes and the high chair.

"Oh, you poor kid!" Katie said. She grabbed some paper towels and wiped off his face and clothes. *Oh, no!* she told herself. *He's sick! Maybe that's why he didn't want to eat the other day.*

Justin's eyes shone with tears. His little mouth turned down at the corners. "Bad! Bad!" he mumbled.

"It's okay, Justin. I'll get you cleaned up," she reassured him. But, as much as she loved him, Katie couldn't bring herself to give him a hug—not until she got him cleaned up.

Katie helped him down from the high chair and led him into the bathroom. She felt his forehead, one of the few clean spots left on his body, but it didn't seem hot to her. In the bathroom, she ran a few inches of warm water in the tub while she carefully pulled his clothes off and found a sponge.

Justin sat very still in the bathwater as Katie wrapped his smelly clothes in a towel. She almost wished he would splash her, like he had the week before. It was scary to see him so quiet.

"How do you feel now, honey?" she asked.

He looked up at her without answering. *What if he has something serious?* Katie worried. *I wish Anne had told me where she was going, so I could call her. This seems like an emergency. I guess I'll call Mr. Stuart.*

Katie squeezed the big sponge full of soapy water over Justin's shoulder. "I think you're all clean now, honey," she told him. She helped him stand up in the tub. That's when she saw the bruise.

It was a round purple mark on his left hip, about three inches wide. Four long marks extended out from the big round one, back toward his rear end.

He must have fallen on one of his toys, Katie decided. Then she stared at the mark for a minute. *That bruise has a really weird shape,* she told herself. She held her right hand up to it. It fit. *No,* Katie thought as she shook her head, *that can't be a handprint. It's just an ordinary bruise. Kids get bruises all the time, in all different shapes.*

But Justin did say his daddy spanks him, Katie remembered. *For crying, wasn't it? Maybe Mr. Stuart doesn't realize how strong he is. I wonder if Anne knows about this bruise.*

Justin looked at her as she knelt next to the bathtub. "Dusty eat dinner up. Dusty good boy?" he asked.

She kissed his damp cheek. "Yes, Dusty is a very good boy," she agreed. He smiled happily and put his short little arms around her neck and hugged her.

Katie wrapped him in a thick towel and took him to his room for some clean clothes. *I wish I knew where Anne is,* she thought. *I guess I still should call Mr. Stuart and tell him about Justin throwing up. But I won't mention the bruise. I'm probably wrong anyway. I can't believe he would hit his little boy so hard.*

She gave Justin a wooden puzzle and sat him down on the kitchen floor, away from the messy high chair. "Just sit here a minute while I call Daddy," she said.

It seemed like two weeks before Mr. Stuart came to the phone.

"Yes?" said a deep voice.

She swallowed. "Uh, this is Katie Weber," she began.

"Yes, Miss Weber, what can I do for you?" he asked.

"Uh, well, I'm not a customer. I'm Justin's baby-sitter. I don't know where Anne—Mrs. Stuart—is."

"Well, I'm not sure where she is either," he said. "What seems to be the problem?"

"Uh, Justin's sick. At least I think so. He . . . uh . . . threw up," she finally blurted out.

"Can you tell if he has a fever?" Mr. Stuart asked.

"I don't think he does," Katie said. "He's just sitting here playing with a puzzle."

Mr. Stuart was quiet for a few seconds. She could hear his secretary telling him something. When he came back, he was talking faster. "Well, it sounds like Justin's fine now. Anne should be home soon. She'll take care of him then. Thanks for calling."

"Uhh . . ." Katie began, but Mr. Stuart had already hung up.

He must be very busy, Katie told herself.

Katie had just finished cleaning up the highchair, holding her breath the whole time, when she heard Anne pull into the driveway. Justin was still sitting on the floor nearby, playing with another puzzle.

"How's everything here?" Anne asked as she came in from the garage. She was carrying another shopping bag.

"Mommy!" Justin's face lit up when he saw

his mother, and he rushed to hug her knees.

Anne smiled and patted his back. Then she reached into her bag and pulled out a big box. "Here's something for my favorite boy!" she said as she opened it. Inside was a big red fire truck. Justin let out a whoop, plopped down on the floor, and started to play with it.

Anne turned to Katie and smiled. "Katie, I'm sorry I was so mad when I left. I feel a lot better now." She glanced down at her son. "Some days it's not easy to stay home with a two-year-old, especially one who touches things he isn't supposed to touch." Her voice suddenly had a sharp edge to it. Justin looked up at her with worried eyes.

Katie hoped that Anne didn't mean the crystal fawn. "I think Justin might be sick," Katie said quickly. "He threw up his dinner."

"He threw up?" Mrs. Stuart repeated. She quickly knelt down in front of Justin and tipped his face up so she could see it. "Are you sick, honey? Don't you feel well?" She felt his forehead.

"No, no sick, Mom." Justin shook his head. Then he wriggled out of her hands and went back to his new truck.

Anne stood up. "Do you think I should take him to the doctor?" she asked Katie in a worried voice. "Oh, I wish my mother were here! She always knew what to do before! We live so far away now!" She rubbed her forehead as if she had a headache.

"We could call Mrs. Wilson next door," Katie suggested. "She has three little kids. She'd know what to do."

Anne pressed her lips together and shook her head. "I can't call someone I don't know and ask if my little boy is sick."

She glanced down at her son, who was happily pushing the fire truck around the kitchen floor and making siren noises. "I guess he looks okay," Anne said, half to herself.

Katie nodded, but she wasn't at all sure.

Anne took a big breath. "I can handle this," she said. "Thanks for coming today. I don't know what I'd do without you." She gave Katie a tired smile. "Hey, your shirt is wet!"

"Well, Justin needed a bath," Katie mumbled.

"Oh! Let me get the shirt you left the other day," Anne offered.

"Okay," Katie said. "I still have your shirt at home, too. I meant to bring it back today. I'm sorry!"

"No problem," Anne said. "In fact," she said as she started walking toward her bedroom, "I've got a couple here I was thinking of giving away. Maybe you'd like them."

Katie followed Anne into a huge walk-in closet in her bedroom. One side was clearly for Mr. Stuart. A row of dark suits hung there, along with about twenty shirts in pastel shades. Racks of dress and casual shoes sat on the floor.

On the other side of the closet hung clothes of all colors and patterns. Some of the clothes, Katie noticed, still had store tags on them. A shelf over the hanging clothes was piled high with shoeboxes on one end and, on the other, clear plastic boxes filled with sweaters.

"How about this one?" Anne asked. "Would this fit you?" She pulled out a shirt striped in soft shades of lavender and pink and held it up to Katie.

"It's beautiful!" Katie exclaimed.

"Here's a beige one that's been around for a while," Anne said, handing another shirt to Katie.

"Are you sure you don't want these?" Katie asked uncertainly.

"They're all yours!" Anne said with a smile. "In fact, I think you are just the right size for one more thing," Anne said. She hunted through the clothes in the back of the closet and pulled out a jeans jacket. "Here! This was my favorite, but I want you to have it. I'm too old for this now."

"Oh, wow!" was all Katie could say. Most of the kids at school had jeans jackets. But because Katie knew her mother couldn't afford one, she'd never asked for one.

Katie thanked Anne, gave Justin a quick hug as he played with his truck, and hurried home to call Liz.

"A jeans jacket, too?" Liz repeated in amazement. "Mrs. Stuart must be really nice! You sure are lucky, Katie Weber. Baby-sitting Justin *and* getting those new clothes!"

"Well, the baby-sitting didn't go so well today," Katie told her. "Justin threw up."

"Yuck!" Liz said. "Do you think he's sick?"

"I'm not sure," Katie admitted. "He did eat his dinner awfully fast. Maybe that's what did it. I think I'll call Anne tomorrow night and make sure he's okay."

"Good idea!" Liz said. "Whoops! I'm late. I was supposed to be at the Watermans' house 15 minutes ago. Mr. Waterman is going to pay me to weed his garden!"

A little later, as Katie set the table for dinner, she remembered the bruise on Justin's hip. *Maybe I should talk to Mom about it,* she worried, *just to see what she thinks. But Mom's so busy with everything. She has enough to worry about. Besides, I'm getting carried away. All kids get bruises. Besides, no one would hurt*

46

a little kid like Justin on purpose, especially parents like the Stuarts.

There's nothing to worry about.

Except your history paper that's due tomorrow, Katie reminded herself. *I'd be happy if I never ever heard about the Civil War again,* she decided.

Seven

AT lunch on Wednesday Katie waited for Liz at their usual table. She could barely keep her eyes open. *Working on that paper until midnight was one thing,* Katie thought sleepily. *But I also didn't need Mom worrying this morning about my staying up so late. She was wrong, anyway. I wouldn't have had the paper finished any earlier if I didn't have my baby-sitting job.*

"Ugh!" Liz said as she slowly eased her body down on the seat next to Katie. "The backs of my legs hurt like crazy! I'll never weed a garden again! And look at my poor hand!"

Liz held up her right hand. There was an ugly red blister in the center of her palm from the handle of the spade Liz had used in the Watermans' flower bed.

"One good thing might come from this,

though," Liz said as she inspected her hand. "I can't very well take my math test this afternoon, can I? I probably can't even hold a pencil with this blister."

"And besides that, you didn't study, right?" Katie asked with a grin.

"Well!" Liz looked up at Katie and pretended to be insulted. Then Liz took a closer look at her friend. "Katie, you look like you studied *all* night! Wait, I remember—your history paper's due today, right?"

Katie nodded and sighed. "I thought I'd never get it done."

Liz stared at Katie for a minute. "Is that all that's wrong?" she asked.

Katie put her sandwich down. "I saw a weird bruise on Justin yesterday. On his rear end. I keep thinking about it. It looked like a handprint."

"Maybe his mom or dad spanked him a little too hard," Liz suggested.

"But spanking shouldn't leave a mark, should it?" Katie asked.

"I guess not," Liz agreed. "If it really is a handprint, though, I bet it was an accident. The Stuarts seem so nice. Which reminds me—that shirt looks great on you!" Katie was wearing the lavender-striped one Anne had given her.

"Maybe it isn't even a handprint," Liz went on. "Maybe Justin fell on a toy with a funny shape."

"You're probably right," Katie said slowly. *I hope so, anyway,* she thought.

"Elizabeth Humphrey, the time has come!" It was Kenny, standing next to their table.

"Are you going to the dance with me or not?" he asked. "Hundreds of girls will cry themselves to sleep tonight if you say yes. But we'll just have to take that chance!"

Liz looked up at him in surprise. Then she bit her lip for a second and glanced around. Katie figured she was checking to see if Mike was nearby.

"Kenny, didn't I tell you?" Liz said. "Of course I'll go with you!"

Kenny gave her a big smile. "I knew it! I'm irresistible!" He turned and disappeared into the crowd.

But Liz was already frowning. "How am I going to tell Mike, Katie? He's such a nice guy! Help me!"

Just then the bell rang, and Mike hurried over to walk Liz to class. Katie saw a look of panic in Liz's eyes. Katie gathered her books and started toward her next class, wondering what in the world Liz would tell Mike about the dance.

That evening, Katie called Anne to see how Justin was feeling.

"Hello?" Mr. Stuart answered.

"Uh, this is Katie Weber . . . Justin's baby-sitter?" Katie said.

"Yes, Katie."

"Uh, is Anne—Mrs. Stuart—there?" she asked hopefully.

"No, she's at the grocery store. Can I help you?"

"Well, I was thinking about Justin," she said, "and, uh, I wondered how he was doing today. I mean, did he get sick again, like yesterday?"

"Sick? No, Justin's not sick—just stubborn," Mr. Stuart told her. "Sometimes I think Anne lets him get away with too much."

Katie suddenly had a sick feeling in her own stomach. She had never seen Justin get away with anything—not in front of his mother, anyway.

"Justin is always so good for me!" she said quickly.

"Well, Anne seems to think you're a great baby-sitter. Thanks for calling, Katie. Bye, now," Mr. Stuart said as he hung up.

Katie went up to her bedroom and flopped down on her bed. *You should be happy,* she told herself as she stared at the ceiling. *Anne really likes you. You can keep baby-sitting Justin. Maybe when you've saved a little more money, your mom will let you put that dress on layaway before someone else buys it. You'll wear the dress to the Spring Dance, and Scott won't be able to take his eyes off you.*

Anyway, all kids get bruises. There's nothing to worry about.

* * * * *

When Katie got to the Stuarts' Thursday afternoon, travel brochures were spread on the kitchen table. "Are you going on vacation?" she asked Anne.

Anne nodded. "We thought Justin would get a big kick out of Disney World. The only problem is, his dad wants us to be able to go places without Justin, too." She smiled at Katie. "Could you come with us, if your mom doesn't mind? We're going the last week in July."

"Disney World! I'd love to! I never thought I'd get there!" *Wait till I tell Mom!* Katie thought. *And Liz and Scott!*

Anne picked up her purse and started out. "Where is Justin?" Katie asked as Anne headed for the door.

"He's playing in his room," Anne answered.

"His dinner's in the refrigerator. Make sure he eats it all."

"Is he feeling okay today?" Katie asked.

"Oh, he's fine now. I still don't know what was wrong with him on Tuesday," Anne said. "See you later. I'm going to do some errands downtown."

Katie nodded and walked back to Justin's room, but Justin's room was empty. "Justin, I'm here!" she called. "Where are you?" But there was no answer. Katie checked the two other bedrooms and walked back toward the kitchen. *I'll bet he's hiding from me,* she thought.

Then she noticed that the basement door was open just a crack. *Oh, no!* Katie thought. "Justin?" she called.

She swallowed hard and pushed the door open. It was so dark she couldn't see a thing. Katie flipped the light switch. He wasn't there! Justin hadn't fallen to the bottom of the steps after all! Katie leaned against the doorway and tried to catch her breath.

Where is he, then? she wondered. "Justin! You come out right now! This isn't a game!"

Katie hurried through the house, looking under beds and opening closets. "Justin! You better come out! I mean it!"

But there was still no answer. She ran outside and circled the house, calling.

Back inside the house, Katie could feel her heart pounding in her chest. *I've got to call someone,* she decided. *Justin might be in real trouble.* She took a deep breath to help her think better. *I can't call Anne—she could be anywhere. Maybe I should call Mr. Stuart,* she thought. *Maybe Justin's done this before. His dad might know where he's hiding . . . if he is hiding,* Katie reminded herself.

She reluctantly reached for the phone in the Stuarts' bedroom. Just as she started dialing, she heard a giggle.

"Justin!" she yelled. The sound had come from the bathroom. She hurried in and pulled the shower curtain aside. Empty. Then she yanked open the linen closet. There were only towels, folded neatly on the shelves. *I already looked in this bathroom anyway,* she told herself. *He wasn't in here then and he isn't in here now.*

Then she heard another giggle. She turned toward the sound. It came from the cabinet under the sink! Katie pulled the cabinet door open. Justin had wedged himself in under the pipes that drained the sink. He grinned up at her.

"Here me!" he said gleefully.

Katie grabbed his arm and pulled him out,

knocking over several bottles of shampoo in the cabinet.

"Don't you ever do that again!" she shouted at him.

Justin's smile disappeared. His eyes grew big and round.

"Dusty sorry. No hide," he promised quickly.

"You scared me to death!" she told him. Hot tears rushed to her eyes, and she tried to blink them away. Then she noticed how tightly she was holding his arm. Katie let go, and Justin collapsed in a limp pile on the floor. When he looked up at her, his eyes also glistened with tears.

"Oh, I'm sorry!" Katie said. "I was just so worried about you." She sat on the floor and pulled him onto her lap. He put his short little arms around her neck, and they hugged each other. Katie took a couple of deep breaths. *You'd better pull yourself together,* she told herself firmly, *or you'll be the one leaving bruises.*

Just to make sure, Katie pulled Justin's sleeve up. His arm was a little red where she had grabbed him. *Oh, no! I didn't mean to hurt him at all,* she insisted to herself. *I was just so worried!*

"Justin, how would you like to play with the

pots and pans?" Katie offered in a shaky voice. Within two seconds he was out of her lap and running for the kitchen. As Katie straightened the bathroom cabinet, she heard the first *CLANG!!!* By the time Anne got home, Katie had the worst headache of her life.

Eight

"WELL, we have to ask *your* neighbors, Katie," Liz explained. They were standing in Katie's backyard. "I already asked most of my neighbors, and they don't want their dogs washed. They must like them dirty, I guess."

"But . . ." Katie began.

"Don't worry! Look, we've got the tub of water all ready and your mom's old towels and my very own bottle of shampoo. What can go wrong?" Liz shrugged her shoulders.

"But I never gave a dog a bath before!" Katie objected.

"I'll show you how!" Liz promised. "You just wait here. I'll go get our first dog!"

Why do I let Liz talk me into these things? Katie asked herself. *There must be other, safer ways Liz can earn the last few dollars she needs to buy her dress.*

Ten minutes later, just when Katie had decided her neighbors must like their dogs dirty too, Liz came back around the corner of the house. She was pulling two dogs, both on leashes.

"I thought we'd do two at once and save time!" Liz called to Katie. "This is Wolf." She nodded toward the bigger dog, a huge German shepherd. "And this is Bitsy." Bitsy was a shaggy little dog that Katie knew lived across the street. Bitsy yipped happily when she heard her name.

Just then, Wolf spotted the tub of water and stopped dead in his tracks. Bitsy, who was too short to see what was in the tub, seemed to think Wolf wanted to play. She started running in circles around the big dog, yapping excitedly.

In seconds the two leashes were hopelessly tangled. Bitsy's leash now held her within inches of the shepherd's long nose. Wolf finally seemed to get annoyed at Bitsy's yipping and started barking himself, very loudly. Bitsy's eyes grew big and round, and she started to whine.

"Thank goodness Mom's at the grocery store," Katie shouted to Liz over the noise. They frantically tried to separate the leashes before the big dog ate the little one. "She might think we have a problem here."

"She'd be right!" said a deep voice. Mr. Evans, Bitsy's owner, had appeared from nowhere. Bitsy started yapping hysterically and struggling against the twisted leashes, trying to get to him.

Mr. Evans unhooked his terrified dog from her leash, picked her up, and quickly untangled the leashes. At a glance from him, Wolf stopped barking and sat down. Mr. Evans looked at the girls over the top edge of his glasses.

"Uh, sorry . . ." Katie began. But the look on his face told her there was nothing she could say to make things better. He turned and left.

"Well," Liz said, "who could have guessed such cute dogs would be so noisy?"

"Liz . . ." Katie said in a tired voice.

"Now don't get discouraged," Liz said reassuringly. "We still have Wolf here." She patted the shepherd's head as he sat panting. Katie wondered how that long pink tongue ever would fit back in his mouth. She could see rows of pointed teeth.

Liz tugged on the dog's leash. "Come on, boy, let's get in the water now." Wolf just looked at her and kept panting.

"Let's pick him up and put him in the tub," Liz suggested.

"Wait!" Katie said quickly. She was determined to keep her distance from those teeth. "Liz, tell me the truth. Did you ever give a dog a bath before?"

Liz put her hands on her hips. "There is *nothing* to giving a dog a bath. You soap him up, you rinse him off. We'll just wash him right where he is if he's going to be so stubborn. Here, you hold the leash."

Liz handed the leash to Katie and fished the sponge out of the tub. She plopped it on the dog's back and let the water run down his sides. He turned and looked at her, but didn't seem to mind too much.

"If he would just close his mouth, I would feel better," Katie said.

For the next two or three minutes Wolf sat quietly while Liz got him wet and soapy with the big sponge. "See! This is easy!" she said with a smile.

That's when it happened. Suddenly Wolf bolted away, jerking the leash out of Katie's hands. He shot around the corner of her house and headed for the street, his tongue hanging out as he ran.

As the girls tried to catch him, Wolf raced into the yard of a house halfway down the street. "That's his house!" Liz shouted to Katie.

A woman dressed in white clothes and carrying a tennis racket was heading for her car in the driveway. She heard the commotion and turned just as Wolf leaped.

Oh, no, Katie thought. She stopped running and covered her eyes.

When Katie looked again, the woman had muddy paw prints clear up to her shoulders. She was yelling at the dog, who lay in front of her with his head between his paws.

"We better go explain what happened," Katie said.

Liz nodded dejectedly. "Do you think she'll pay us for washing half of him?"

"Somehow I don't think so," Katie said. Just then, the woman grabbed Wolf by his collar and dragged him inside the house.

"Let's come back later," Liz suggested.

"Only if you promise you'll come with me," Katie said.

"I promise!" Liz crossed her heart. The girls turned around and walked back toward Katie's house.

"Maybe I should try baby-sitting again," Liz said. "It's sure a lot easier than washing dogs."

"You know," Katie said slowly, "sometimes baby-sitting isn't so easy."

"Hey, that doesn't sound good. What happened?" Liz asked. "Did Justin throw up again?" Liz asked with a frown.

"No, but . . ." Katie began.

Just then a red sports car drove past.

"Oh, wow," Liz said with a smile. "Do you ever get to talk to Justin's father? He seems like such a dreamboat!"

Katie frowned. "It's more complicated than you think. . . ."

"True," Liz agreed. "For one thing, he's already married!"

"Liz! That's not what I'm talking about!" Katie said. "I'm still worried about that bruise."

"The one that looked like a handprint?" Liz asked. Katie nodded. Liz looked back at the sports car, which was pulling into the Stuarts' driveway. "Do you . . . do you think his father made that bruise?"

Katie didn't answer. The whole idea did seem crazy. They watched Mr. Stuart get out of his car, walk around it, and help Justin out of his car seat.

Liz shook her head. "He sure doesn't look like he would hit Justin that hard." She turned to Katie. "I really don't think he did. Justin must have just fallen on something.

Katie nodded uncertainly. *That has to be it,* she decided.

Nine

WHEN Anne answered the door Tuesday afternoon, Katie didn't see Justin at first. But as he peeked around his mother's skirt, Katie's breath caught in her throat. His left cheek was black and purple.

Katie swallowed hard. "Hi, Justin," she managed to say.

He smiled up at her. The bruise was partly covered by his shiny blond hair, but that made it look even more out of place.

"Oh, that's right," Anne said. "You haven't seen Justin's boo-boo yet." She picked him up and hugged him. He put his arms around her neck. "He fell out of bed Friday night."

Katie forced herself to smile. *Of course,* she told herself. *Kids do that all the time. Get a hold of yourself, Katie.*

After Anne left, Katie felt somehow trapped in the Stuarts' house.

"How about some fresh air, Justin? Let's go to the park, okay?" she asked.

Justin nodded and smiled. Before they left, though, Katie rooted through his toy chest until she found a baseball cap she had seen him wear one day. "This will keep the sun out of your eyes," she told him. She put it on, turning the brim to shade the left side of his face.

A little later, Katie was pushing Justin on the swings when she heard a familiar voice ask, "Is this swing taken?"

It was Scott, standing behind her, holding Laura by her hand.

"Scott! Hi! Boy, this is a surprise!" Katie pushed her hair back and tried to comb it with her fingers.

She turned to the little girl. "Hi, Laura!" she said cautiously. "Don't you look nice today!" Laura was wearing a little dress with teddy bears dancing around the hem of the skirt. Even though the little girl didn't look at her, Katie thought she saw the corners of Laura's mouth turn up a little.

Scott helped Laura onto a swing and gave her a gentle push. Katie leaned close to him and asked, "How is she doing? I think she almost smiled at me!"

"She's getting along great," he said loudly.

"Right, Laura?" The little girl nodded a little as she sat stiffly in the swing, holding tightly onto the chains at each side. As the swing went a little higher, she started to make high-pitched, singing noises.

Justin heard the noises, too, and twisted in his swing to look at Laura. The wind caught the brim of his baseball cap and blew it off.

"Down, Tatie," Justin called. "Pay in sand now!" Katie lifted Justin down, trying to stay between him and Scott. The little boy hurried over to the park's sandbox.

"Katie!" Scott whispered. She could tell he had seen the bruise. "What happened to Justin?"

"Anne said he fell out of bed," Katie said as convincingly as she could. "Kids do that all the time."

Scott frowned. "Hey, Justin, come on over here for a minute, big boy," he called.

Justin beamed and ran over to Scott, who picked him up to get a better look at the bruise. *It's ugly,* Katie admitted to herself. She turned away and gave Laura's swing a little push.

"Looks like you have a big boo-boo, Justin," Scott said. "How did that happen?"

Justin put his thumb in his mouth.

"Did you fall out of bed?" Katie asked.

The child nodded.

Scott looked at Justin's face for a few seconds. Then he set him down. "Okay, go and play!" Justin smiled up at Scott and raced back to the sandbox.

"That's a bad bruise," Scott said to Katie. "Do you think he really fell out of bed?"

"Sure!" Katie said. "You're so used to hanging around abused kids, you think kids don't ever have accidents!"

"Well, maybe," Scott admitted.

Katie smiled but she didn't feel happy. *I better not tell him about the bruise on Justin's hip last week,* she decided. *He might jump to conclusions, especially since he doesn't know the Stuarts. Justin falls a lot, that's all. Like the time he scraped his knee in the basement,* she reminded herself.

On the way home, Justin told Katie, "T-ba hung'y! T-ba eat!"

As soon as Katie unlocked the Stuarts' front door, Justin ran into his bedroom and came out dragging his teddy bear. He propped the raggedy old bear up in his high chair. "Bow, Tatie! An' 'poon!" Justin demanded.

Katie, smiling, handed Justin his favorite bowl with the bunny in the bottom and his special matching spoon.

"What does the teddy bear like to eat?" she

asked, holding in a giggle.

Justin had climbed on a chair so he could reach his bear. "All dinner!" he answered. "He good ba!"

Justin dipped the spoon in the empty bowl and shoved it at the bear's embroidered mouth. "Eat, ba!" he said seriously. Justin pretended to fill the spoon several more times, but each time he fed the bear, he jammed the spoon harder against its mouth.

By the third or fourth time, Justin was practically stabbing the bear with the spoon. "Eat, ba! Eat!" he shouted.

As Katie watched, a chill ran through her body. She remembered the bruises she had seen in his mouth. Is this how he got them?

"Stop!" Katie yelled. She grabbed the spoon and threw it in the sink. Justin looked up at her in surprise. His face was flushed, and he had a strange look in his eyes.

"Come on, honey," Katie said as calmly as she could. "It's time for *Sesame Street*." She pulled him off the chair and led him into the living room. For the next half hour Katie sat in the corner of the couch with Justin in her lap. He snuggled against her and seemed to be watching the show. Katie just stared at the screen, trying not to think.

A picture hanging on the wall above the

television set caught her eye. It was of the Stuarts at their wedding. Anne looked like an angel in a lacy, white gown with her curly hair falling over her shoulders. Mr. Stuart looked proud and handsome standing beside her in his white tux. They were both smiling. He had his arm around her shoulders. They were a beautiful couple.

I must be imagining things, Katie decided. *Justin just got carried away feeding his teddy bear. That's all.* She smoothed back his silky hair. *No one would have fed Justin that way.*

Too soon, it was Justin's dinnertime. Katie had dreaded it, but he seemed perfectly willing to eat. The only problem was, he wouldn't feed himself.

"Come on," Katie begged. "You eat by yourself all the time!"

But he just put his thumb in his mouth and looked at her with big brown eyes. She tried not to stare at his bruise.

Finally Katie gave up and fed him, slowly, so he wouldn't throw up again. Before each bite, she asked, "Ready for more?"

He would nod and open his mouth. *He looks like a little bird,* Katie told herself, *or a much younger child.* Once he said, "Dusty eat. Daddy lub Dusty."

Katie felt like crying. "Justin, Daddy loves

you whether you eat all your dinner or not." He nodded, but then he opened his mouth again for her to feed him.

That night, Katie had trouble falling asleep. She thought of Jackie, another two-year-old she had watched the summer before. Jackie's favorite word was "MYSELF!" which she shouted at the top of her lungs every time Katie tried to help her. *Jackie would never sit there with her mouth open like a robot,* Katie thought sadly. *But then, Justin didn't use to do that, either.*

It does seem like Justin gets too many bruises, she worried. *And now he won't eat by himself. That's really strange. I'd better talk to my mom about this,* she decided. *Maybe I will tonight, when she gets home from work.*

Today at the park, Scott didn't seem to believe Justin got that bruise falling out of bed, Katie thought. *Maybe I really should tell him about the bruise I saw on Justin's rear end last week . . . and what he did to his teddy bear today. But what if Scott tells his parents? The Dennises might tell the people from the children's social services agency, the same people who took Laura away from her parents. What if they came and took Justin away, too?*

And what if I don't say anything to anyone? Katie thought. *Maybe Mr. Stuart really does hit*

Justin hard enough to leave bruises. What if he gets really mad sometime and breaks his arm? What if he shakes him, like Laura's father shook her? Katie squeezed her eyes shut. *That couldn't happen! Not to Justin!* Tears slipped down her face and made wet spots on her pillow.

What if . . . Katie opened her eyes wide. *What if I said something about the bruises, and Mr. Stuart said they were my fault? Who would people believe—a 14-year-old girl or the vice president of a bank?*

Katie felt her heart pounding in her chest. *Maybe I can handle this myself,* she decided, *without getting a lot of people mixed up in it and making it worse than it is already.*

I'll just talk to Anne. When she realizes what's happening, she'll make her husband stop hurting Justin. I won't tell anyone else, not even Scott or my mom. And I won't mention Justin's bruises to Liz again. Then if I keep babysitting, I can make sure nothing really bad happens to Justin. That's it! No one else will have to know about this. I know I can handle it!

Ten

KATIE spent Wednesday morning trying to decide how she would talk to Anne about Justin's bruises. She planned out several conversations in her head, but so far all of them ended with Anne denying everything and throwing Katie out. *This all seemed so easy last night,* Katie told herself. *I've got to find a way!*

"Well, what do you think?" Liz asked Katie at lunchtime.

"Uh, about what?" Katie asked.

"Calling Kenny and Mike and telling them I have mono and can't go to the dance!" Then Liz leaned forward and looked closely at Katie. "Something's bothering you, Katie. You haven't heard a word I said. Did you have an argument with your mom?"

Katie shook her head. She tried to concentrate on Liz. "I thought you told Kenny you'd go to the dance with him.

"Well . . ." Liz shrugged her shoulders. "I was walking to school with Mike this morning, and he asked about the dance and . . ."

"You told him you'd go to the dance with him, too, right?" Katie asked. Liz nodded sheepishly and looked away. "Liz! You can't have two dates!"

Liz frowned. "I know. Actually I can't go with Mike or Kenny—the other one will feel bad. But if I tell them I'm sick, they'll both ask someone else to the dance and have a good time. I'll just stay home."

"Stay home? After you worked so hard to get the money for your dress?" Katie asked. "You *have* to go."

Liz nodded and pushed crumbs from her sandwich off the table. "This is all my fault. I couldn't make up my mind. I really want to go with both of them, but somehow I don't think that would work out."

Katie stared at her best friend. *I'm probably not going to the dance either,* she wanted to tell Liz. *I probably won't have a dress to wear.*

If I talk to Anne tomorrow about Justin's bruises, she might insist they were all just accidents, Katie told herself. *Then she might be so mad that she won't want me to baby-sit anymore. I'll never be able to earn enough money to buy that dress.*

And much worse, Katie realized, *Justin might keep having "accidents."* She remembered how ugly the bruise looked on his cheek. And she thought about Laura, screaming and pulling her hair. *I have to talk to Anne,* she told herself. *What if something awful happens to Justin because I was too afraid to say anything?*

Katie patted Liz's arm. "Something will work out, Liz. I know it will." *For both of us,* she wanted to add.

Katie was still trying to think of a good way to bring up Justin's bruises when she rang the Stuarts' doorbell Thursday afternoon.

"Hi, Katie!" Anne said cheerfully. "Come on in! Did you ask your mom about coming with us to Disney World?"

The question caught Katie by surprise. "Oh, uh, sure! She says fine!" she answered. *This isn't what you were supposed to say,* Katie warned herself.

"Good! I'll make the reservations today," Anne said.

Just then Justin ran into the kitchen. The bruise on his cheek was an ugly yellow now. *This is it,* Katie told herself, although she still didn't know what she would say. "Anne—"

"Wait till I tell you the big news!" Anne interrupted. "Justin is learning how to use the potty!"

Uh-oh, Katie told herself. *We're really in trouble now.* She tried to smile. Anne looked so proud.

"Now, Justin, while I'm shopping, you tell Katie when you have to go to the potty," Anne reminded him as she headed for the door. "No more accidents. Remember what Daddy told you." Katie saw the warning look that Anne gave her son.

Justin nodded and turned to Katie. "I big boy! Dusty wear pants!" He pointed at his thick, white training pants.

Anne was barely out the door before Justin was standing in a puddle of his own making.

Katie groaned inside, but she knew it wasn't Justin's fault. She didn't think little boys his age were supposed to be toilet trained. She left the pants in a soggy pile on the kitchen floor and quickly led Justin to the toilet. As soon as she lifted him on it, he announced, "No more!"

Katie closed her eyes. It was going to be a long afternoon. "How about a diaper?" she suggested with an encouraging smile.

"No!" he insisted. His eyes got big and round. "Dusty wear pants!"

"But Dusty . . . I mean, Justin . . ." Katie began. Then she shook her head. Maybe he would do better this time. She put another pair of training pants on him and rinsed the wet ones out in the bathtub. *If I dry these in the clothes dryer,* she decided, *no one will know. The fewer reasons for Mr. Stuart to be mad at Justin, the better.*

Katie squeezed the water out of the pants and went to check on Justin. He was in his room, hunting for something in his toy box. *This is my chance,* Katie thought. She hurried through the kitchen and down into the basement, tossed the wet pants in the dryer, flipped it on, and raced back upstairs.

"Tatie!" Justin was calling from his bedroom. "Look! Nice!"

"Oh, no!" Katie said in a choked voice. Justin had drawn on the wall beside his dresser. It was a big, lopsided circle with two smaller circles in it.

"See?" he said proudly. "My daddy!" He held a fat red crayon in his hand.

Katie grabbed the crayon out of his hand and scraped at the marks on the wall with her fingernail. Some of the red came off, but she could still see Justin's handiwork.

Katie turned to Justin. She couldn't hide her anger. "You're not supposed to draw on the walls!"

His eyes were as big as saucers. "I sorry. No more!" He shook his head and dropped the crayon. She could see his tears start to gather.

"Justin," Katie said through clenched teeth, "would you please sit quietly somewhere for a minute?" He nodded and plopped down right where he was.

Katie got as much crayon off as she could. Then she moved his dresser over about two feet so it covered the marks. *Maybe the Stuarts won't notice—at least for a while,* she prayed.

By the time Anne came home, Katie had rinsed and dried another pair of training pants and tried her best to sponge up a wet spot on the carpet in the living room. She had managed to get Justin to go once—a few drops, anyway—in the toilet. Katie also fed Justin his dinner, which he ate like a baby bird again, stopping every few bites to remind Katie what a good boy he was.

"Justin used the potty!" Katie announced as soon as Anne came in the door. She hoped Justin would not tell his mother about the other things.

Anne scooped him up and gave him a big kiss. "Great! Wait till I tell Daddy!" She turned to Katie. "Greg really is pleased that Justin seems to be calming down now." Katie's stomach turned over. "We think you've helped a lot, so this week I want to give you a little extra." She pulled out her wallet.

Anne handed Katie $15. "I don't know what I'd do without you, Katie," she said. She reached over and gave Katie a quick hug.

Katie looked at the money in her hand, a ten and a five. "Uhh, I can't . . ." she began.

"I want you to have that," Anne insisted. "I know you're saving for a dress for that dance. In fact, if you're available, we'd like to have you watch Justin a week from this Saturday night, too. Greg and I are going to his boss' house for dinner. Can you do it? The extra money might buy half a pair of shoes!" Anne smiled.

Katie opened her mouth, but no words came out. All she could do was nod. *You coward!* she screamed inwardly at herself. *You have to say something about the bruises to Anne! She has to make her husband stop hurting Justin!*

"Thanks. See you Tuesday." Katie's throat was so dry it hurt to talk. *Next Tuesday you will talk to her about these bruises, Katie Weber,* she promised herself on the short walk home. *No excuses!*

That night after dinner, Scott came over to study for another history test.

"Well, what was the date of the treaty? Katie?"

Katie blinked. "What?"

"What are you thinking about so hard?" Scott asked.

She forced herself to smile. *Should I tell him?* Katie wondered for the hundredth time. *What would happen? And what if I'm wrong? No,* she finally decided, *it's too big a risk. I can handle this myself.*

After Scott left, though, Katie hurried upstairs to call Liz.

"I need to talk to you," Katie said nervously. "Will you promise not to tell anyone what I tell you?"

Liz was eating something crunchy, like an apple. "Sure, you can count on me. What's so important?"

"It's . . . it's about Justin," Katie started. She could feel her heart thumping in her chest. "Remember the bruise I told you about, the one that looked like a handprint?"

"I remember, but. . . ." Liz said.

Katie took a big breath. "Well, there's another one now. I'm really worried," she whispered. She told Liz about the bruise on Justin's face. "And one day last week he was pretending to feed his teddy bear, but he kept stabbing him with a spoon. . . ."

"Wait, Katie," Liz interrupted. "All kids get bruises! And worse! Remember when I was baby-sitting Timmy Grant and he fell and hit his head on the coffee table? He needed nine stitches!"

"Yes, but . . ." Katie said.

"Well, maybe I didn't tell you what happened when his mom and I got to the emergency room," Liz said. "The doctor asked both of us lots of questions about how it happened. I know she thought one of us hit him. It took a long time for his mom and me to convince the doctor it was an accident, but it was! Accidents happen all the time!"

"But Justin has so many bruises!" Katie insisted.

"Katie, Mr. Stuart is the vice president of a bank, not an animal!" Liz reminded her. "He's got an important job, lots of money, a beautiful wife, and he's gorgeous. Why would he hurt his little boy?"

Later that night, Katie lay awake again. *Maybe Liz is right after all,* she thought. *People like Mr. Stuart just don't beat up their kids. He's not like Laura's father, who was probably mad at everyone all the time. I've got to stop imagining things before I cause some real trouble.*

Eleven

" JUSTIN isn't allowed in the living room anymore," Anne said as soon as she opened the door for Katie on Tuesday. Anne already had her purse and car keys in her hand. "His dinner's in the refrigerator. I just hope he's better for you than he was for me!" She turned and hurried out. She didn't even stop to pick up her jacket lying on the chair.

Justin sat in the corner of the kitchen, fingering some colored rings that fit over a peg. He didn't look up.

"Oh, Justin," Katie said softly. "What happened now?" She knelt beside him and rubbed his back. He was wearing diapers again. The bruise on his cheek had faded some more, but she could still see it.

"Bad boy," he mumbled. Katie tried to hug him, but he winced and pulled away.

She swallowed hard. Oh, please, she prayed,

let there be no more bruises. "What hurts, honey?" she whispered.

"Dusty bad." She could hardly hear him.

Katie gently rubbed Justin's arms and legs, trying to figure out where he hurt. When she touched his upper arm, he pulled away sharply and whimpered.

Katie gently pulled up Justin's sleeve a few inches. His arm was dotted with purple circles. She checked his other arm. It was covered with the same dark circles. Katie turned away and took several deep breaths. Then she slowly eased his shirt off.

Katie sat back on her heels and stared at the shirtless little boy. Justin held up a red ring for Katie to see, then he began to put it on its peg. Katie covered her face with her hands and thought hard.

This is real. I can't pretend anymore that nothing is happening. This is not my imagination. Katie planted a kiss on Justin's forehead and stood up.

She reached for the phone and dialed her mother's number at work. "I'm sorry," said the receptionist. "Your mother is in a meeting for the rest of the afternoon."

Then Katie tried Liz. There was no answer. She thought of Scott. He'd know what to do.

"Sit right there," she told Justin as she

searched for Scott's number in the phone book. She dialed Scott's house with one hand and bent down to smooth Justin's hair with the other.

Scott answered the phone on the second ring.

"Um, Scott . . ." Katie said, her voice shaky.

"Katie . . . what's wrong?" Scott asked.

"It's . . . could you please come over to the Stuarts' right now? I need help."

"Sure, I'll be right there," Scott said, and hung up without even saying good-bye.

Within minutes, Scott was at the Stuarts' front door. Katie led him back to the kitchen where Justin was still playing on the floor.

"Hi, Justin!" Scott called. Justin, still shirtless, glanced up and smiled a little. Then he went back to slowly stacking the rings on the peg, being very careful to put the biggest one on the bottom and the rest in order. When it was full, he dumped them off and started again.

Scott motioned Katie into the living room.

"It looks like someone grabbed his arms, hard," Scott told her quietly. "Maybe they shook him." He searched Katie's eyes.

"Shook him?" The words caught in her throat. "No, that can't be! Not Justin!"

"Katie, how could he fall and hurt both arms

the same way?" Scott asked.

Katie swallowed hard. Her eyes darted around the room. That's when she noticed the crystal buck standing on the table by himself. *Oh, Justin,* Katie thought.

"What's going on, Katie?" Scott looked very serious now. "You have to tell me. Justin may be in danger."

Katie stared into Scott's eyes for a minute. Then she nodded. Whispering so Justin wouldn't hear, she told Scott about the other bruises. Just as she was telling him how Justin forced his teddy bear to eat, a car pulled into the driveway.

"Oh, no!" Katie said in alarm. "It must be Anne—or maybe Mr. Stuart! I'm not supposed to have anyone here unless I ask!"

"But this is different," Scott said.

The door to the garage opened, and Anne rushed in. "Katie, I forgot my . . ." She stopped when she saw Scott. "Oh! I didn't know. . . ."

"Uh, this is Scott," Katie said quickly. "We study together. Remember?"

"Yes, but I didn't know he was going to be here." Anne clearly was not happy to see Scott. Then she glanced down at Justin, who still had his shirt off. The bruises screamed to be noticed.

Anne raised her chin and pressed her lips together. "What's going on here?" she asked.

"Those bruises . . ." Katie began. *This isn't how I planned this*, she thought in a panic. *This is all wrong!*

"It looks like someone has grabbed Justin hard enough to leave those bruises on him," Scott said firmly. "Katie is worried that your husband is hurting your son."

"Well, I don't think that's any of your business!" Anne told Scott.

"But what about that bruise on his face?" Katie asked. "And the one the week before last, on his bottom? It was shaped like a hand. Maybe Mr. Stuart doesn't realize how strong he is!"

"My husband has never laid a hand on Justin!" Anne exploded. Then her tone changed. "I wonder what you two were really doing in this house together." She turned to Scott. "How many times have you been here before?"

"Never!" Scott said. "Katie called me over here today because she was worried about Justin."

Anne looked at Katie. The woman's eyes were wide with anger. "Well, I just wonder if her mother will believe that!"

"My mother trusts me!" Katie insisted.

"Well, I don't! Not anymore!" Anne grabbed Justin's shirt off the kitchen table and put it on him. Katie saw him wince. *Stop!* she wanted to yell. *Stop hurting that little boy!*

"As a matter of fact," Anne said. "Justin *has* had more bruises lately, now that I think about it." She stared up at Katie. "Ever since you started watching him!"

"No!" *This is a nightmare!* Katie thought.

"It's time for both of you to go," Anne told them. "For good!" Her eyes seemed to burn through Katie.

Tears filled Katie's eyes and made everything blurry. She could barely see Justin sitting in the corner with his head down, squeezing one of the colored rings.

Scott took her hand and they left.

"Is your mother home?" he asked as they reached the sidewalk. Katie just shook her head. Her throat was so tight from trying not to cry that she couldn't talk. "Then we'd better go to my house," Scott said.

As they walked toward his house, Katie tried to blink her tears away. Finally, her breathing evened out enough so she could talk. "Maybe I made a big mistake today. I shouldn't have called you. I shouldn't have said anything."

"From what I've seen and heard, Justin isn't

safe in that house," Scott said.

"Maybe," she admitted. "But now it's even worse. If Anne tells her husband what just happened, Mr. Stuart might blame Justin and hit him more. Maybe he'll end up like Laura!" Katie put her hands over her face, but she couldn't keep her sobs back.

They had reached Scott's house. His mom came out of the kitchen to say hello, but then she saw Katie's face. "What's the matter?" she asked in alarm.

Scott led Katie to the couch and made her sit down. Then he told his mother about Justin's bruises and what had just happened at the Stuarts'. As he talked, Laura wandered into the room and sat on the floor near them, making noises to her doll.

When Scott finished, Mrs. Dennis sat quietly for a minute. Finally she said, "I think we need some guidance here. I'll call someone who can help."

"Wait!" Katie yelled as Mrs. Dennis reached for the phone. She hugged herself to keep from panicking. "Who are you going to call?"

"Just some people who know about these things. You need to talk to somebody," Mrs. Dennis answered.

"It's the people from the agency, right? The ones who gave you Laura?" Katie asked in a shaky voice. "Don't call them!"

"I have to call, Katie," she said softly. "As a foster parent, I'm required by law to report possible child abuse. And as a mother, I have to." She looked down at Laura and nodded to herself. "All of us have to. Anyway, I'm going to call a special caseworker, someone I know and like very much. She can decide whether that little boy is really in danger."

"But they might take Justin away!" Katie objected. Her whole body began to shake.

"They don't always do that," Mrs. Dennis explained, "but they do check up on reports."

Katie turned to Scott. "I was afraid this would happen!" She stood up. "Just forget I was here today, please! Everything is okay!" She held her chin higher and moved toward the door. "I just got carried away!"

Mrs. Dennis looked at Scott. He shook his head. "I saw those bruises on Justin's arms, Katie. They were not an accident. And what about that bruise on his face? How did he really get that?"

"This isn't easy for anyone, Katie. But you can't wait until he has a broken bone . . . or worse," Mrs. Dennis added. "Justin needs you to help him. Now." She began to dial the phone.

My whole nightmare came true! she told

herself. *And Scott's mom knows now. She'll tell the agency people even if I don't.*

Someone at the agency answered the phone. Mrs. Dennis explained why she was calling and handed the phone to Katie. Katie had to hold it with both hands to keep from dropping it.

Twelve

"KATIE," a soft voice said, "I'm Mrs. Musgrove. Please tell me what you think is happening with this child you baby-sit." Katie tried to give her just the barest details, but the caseworker kept asking questions.

"The first bruise you noticed, the one on his rear end—how big was it? What did it look like?" the caseworker asked.

Katie swallowed. "It was round mostly . . . but there were three or four long marks coming out from it."

"I see," Mrs. Musgrove said. "Did it remind you of anything?"

"A handprint," Katie whispered.

"And the bruises on the child's arms—how do you think that happened?"

"Maybe he fell," Katie suggested, although she didn't believe it herself. Not anymore.

"Children do fall a lot," the caseworker agreed, "but no one can fall and get little round bruises on the tops of both arms."

I think you're right, Katie agreed silently.

Finally, Mrs. Musgrove asked the hardest question. "Who do you think is hurting this little boy—Justin?"

"The only one it could be is his father," Katie said. "But he's the vice president of a bank!"

"It doesn't really matter what kind of job he has," she said. "Or how much money he has. All kinds of people abuse their kids—rich people and poor people."

"But why?" Katie asked again in confusion. "Justin tries so hard to be good! Why would Mr. Stuart hit him like that?" She wished she could hug Justin right then and tell him he *was* a good boy and that she loved him! Katie brushed her tears away with her hand.

"Adults abuse kids for lots of reasons," Mrs. Musgrove said. "Most parents treat their children just the way they were treated as kids. You see, child abuse is a cycle. Maybe Mr. Stuart's father beat him and he thinks that's the way fathers are supposed to get kids to behave."

"Not all parents do that," Katie couldn't remember her mother ever hitting her.

"That's true," the caseworker agreed, "but lots of parents lose their temper at one time or another—when they're tired or under a lot of stress. They might hit a child out of anger then, but they are immediately sorry and make sure it doesn't happen again."

Katie thought of the day Justin hid from her in the bathroom cabinet. She remembered how tightly she had held his arm. *I almost left bruises on him myself that day,* she realized.

"From what you say," Mrs. Musgrove went on, "Justin has been abused several times already. It sounds as if the abuse might be getting worse. Has he been acting any different lately?"

At first Katie didn't answer. *If I tell her the truth, it will make everything seem worse,* she thought. *If I pretend he's the same. . . .* She thought of how sad Justin had looked, sitting in the corner of the kitchen with his head down.

"He's quieter now," Katie finally said, "and he won't feed himself anymore."

Mrs. Musgrove didn't say anything for a second. Katie guessed she was writing everything down. "I really appreciate you telling me these things, Katie," she said at last.

"What . . . what are you going to do?" Katie asked in a whisper.

"By law I have to investigate this report within 24 hours," she explained. "After I talk with the family and look at the bruises you saw on Justin, I'll decide what would be best for him."

Maybe the bruises will fade by then, Katie prayed. *The caseworker will see that I just exaggerated and she won't take Justin away.* Then a fearful thought gripped her. "Will the Stuarts know who called you?"

"We never tell parents who called us," Mrs. Musgrove said.

"But they'll know it was me!" Katie said in a choked voice. "Oh, please don't go there!" she begged. "Everything will be all right! I'm sure it will!"

"Katie, you were right to tell me about Justin," Mrs. Musgrove said softly. "I can help him, if he needs help."

"But what if he doesn't?" Katie asked in desperation. "What if I'm wrong?"

"You were still right to call. It's worth the chance, believe me. Abused children sometimes die because no one wants to 'tell' on the parents. You may have saved Justin's life," the caseworker said. "Anyway, this isn't your problem now, Katie. We'll take care of it from this point on. You did the best thing."

"I hope so!" Katie said in a choked voice.

"Katie," Mrs. Musgrove added, "those bruises on Justin's arms were probably caused by someone shaking him. Do you know what can happen if a small child is shaken?"

Katie nodded, but she couldn't answer. She put her hand over her mouth so the caseworker wouldn't hear her crying. Mrs. Dennis took the phone from her and thanked Mrs. Musgrove for helping.

Scott held Katie's hand as he walked her home. Neither one of them talked. Mrs. Weber was waiting in the kitchen when they got there. "Katie, where have you—" Her angry look changed to a worried one when she saw her daughter's pale face.

Katie turned to Scott. "I need to talk to my mom now."

He nodded and squeezed her hand. As soon as he left, Katie told her mother what had happened.

Mrs. Weber was stunned. "I had no idea you were so worried! Why didn't you tell me all along what was going on? I could have helped!"

"I knew you had enough on your mind, Mom, so I . . . I didn't want to bother you with my problems. I really thought I could handle it myself," Katie admitted. "I was wrong." A tear slid down her cheek. "There's no other way I could have stopped Mr. Stuart from hurting Justin."

"I'm glad you talked to the caseworker. She'll make sure Justin is safe." Mrs. Weber wiped Katie's tears away with her dishtowel. "I know this means the end of your baby-sitting there, though," she added, "and I know how much you were counting on that money. You gave up a lot to help Justin. But I know you've done the right thing, no matter what happens tomorrow." Her mother pulled her close, and Katie let her tears fall.

That night, Katie lay in bed trying to reassure herself that she had really done the right thing. *I guess I didn't have a choice,* she finally realized. *If I hadn't done everything I could to help Justin, I really couldn't forgive myself.*

When sleep finally came, Katie dreamed she had just arrived at the Stuarts' to baby-sit. Justin was sitting in the corner of the kitchen again with his head down. When he looked up, his eyes were blank, and he was drooling. She called his name, but he just stared at her.

Thirteen

"**I** wanted to stay home today," Katie told Liz at lunch the next day, "but my mom said I should go to school and try not to think about it."

"It sounds like you did all you could," Liz agreed. "Boy, it's a good thing you were the baby-sitter and not me. I might have just kept quiet so I could make enough money to buy that dress."

Katie shook her head. "No, you wouldn't—not after you saw those bruises. You would have done the same thing." She sighed and looked at her watch. "I wonder if Mrs. Musgrove has gone to the Stuarts' yet. I wonder what she'll decide to do."

"Katie," a deep voice said quietly. They looked up to see Scott towering over them. "Uh, could you come to my house after school?" he asked.

"Do we have a test tomorrow?" Katie asked.

"Not that I know of." He grinned. "I just thought you might like some company after school. Besides, I'm supposed to watch Laura and I might need your expert help."

Katie smiled and nodded. Usually she walked past the Stuarts' house on her way home from school. That was the last thing she wanted to do today.

When he left, Liz grinned and poked Katie in the ribs.

"Oh, Liz," Katie whispered. "He just feels sorry for me. He saw me cry yesterday." She stared at her sandwich. "Maybe I'll tell him this afternoon that I . . . I can't go to the dance after all."

"That reminds me," Liz said. "I still need to tell Mike and Kenny. . . ." Then she was strangely quiet. She bit her lip thoughtfully. "You know what? Maybe I'll tell them the truth—that I can't decide between them, so I can't go to the dance with either one. I'll tell them both to ask someone else. I don't want them to miss the dance because I can't make up my mind."

Liz smiled at her best friend. "Why don't you sleep over at my house the night of the dance? We can keep each other company."

Katie tried to smile, but her face wouldn't do

it. Too much was still on her mind.

After school, Laura walked between Scott and Katie on the way to the park. As soon as the little girl could see the sandbox, though, she ran ahead. She was sitting in the middle of it, dragging her fingers through the sand and chirping to herself, when Scott and Katie caught up. They sat down on a nearby bench to watch her. Twice Scott had to jump up to stop Laura from eating the sand.

"Do you think Mrs. Musgrove will take Justin away?" Katie asked.

"I don't know," he answered. "Mom says the agency just does that if the child is in danger or if the parents don't want the child anymore."

Katie knew that wouldn't be the case with the Stuarts. *Anne really loves Justin. She would never let him go . . . if she has a choice,* Katie thought.

"So who did Liz decide to go to the dance with?" Scott asked.

"Liz isn't going to the dance," she told him. "She couldn't decide between Mike and Kenny, so she's going to tell them both she can't go."

And she isn't the only one who isn't going, Katie thought. *I might as well get this over with.*

"I can't go to the dance either, Scott. You'll

have to ask someone else." Katie looked away so he couldn't see the tears well up in her eyes.

"Why not?" he asked quickly.

Katie took a deep breath and faced him. "Now that I'm not baby-sitting for Justin anymore, I won't have enough money for a dress," she told him.

"Then how about going to a movie instead?" Scott suggested. "You don't need a new dress for that, and I won't have to wear a tux."

Katie looked up at him. "A movie?"

Suddenly Scott frowned. Katie realized he was looking over her shoulder. She turned and her heart almost stopped. Anne was standing there, scowling at them and holding Justin by the hand. The little boy peeked up once, but then he went back to kicking a stone with his sneaker.

At least she still has Justin, Katie thought. *Thank goodness they didn't take him away!* But then Katie thought, *Maybe Mrs. Musgrove hasn't even been to the Stuarts' yet.*

"Are you two patrolling the park, too?" Anne asked sarcastically. "Looking for more abused children to save?"

Laura heard the angry voice and looked at Anne with frightened eyes. Then she started to wail, softly at first, then louder.

Anne turned and stared at Laura. "Now there's a child you should check on. Not a happy kid like Justin!"

"As a matter of fact," Scott said quietly, "this child really was abused."

Laura's scream rose higher. She reached for her hair. Scott hurried to sit beside her in the sandbox. He hugged her, pinning her arms to her sides as his mother had done. Within a minute or two she had quieted, but her wide eyes stayed on Anne.

Katie saw the surprised look on Anne's face. *She didn't know Laura was with us,* Katie realized.

"Laura is a foster child at Scott's house," Katie whispered so neither child could hear. "When she was younger, her father couldn't stand her crying, so he . . . he grabbed her by the shoulders and shook her. . . ." Katie tried to go on, but Anne interrupted.

"So what?" Anne demanded. "Why does she scream like that?"

"Her brain is damaged. The shaking broke little blood vessels in her brain." Katie felt tears gathering in her eyes. "Her father didn't know he was hurting her, so he kept shaking her whenever she cried. The brain damage kept getting worse. . . ."

Katie continued. "Now Laura might never

learn to talk or read or write. She needs a lot of special help."

"He shook her?" Anne repeated. "That's all that happened to her? He just shook her?"

Katie nodded. *It's now or never,* she decided. "I know you love your husband," she whispered to Anne, "but you can't let him do the same thing to Justin."

Anne slowly sat down on the bench, hugging herself. Her face was pale. "Go play in the sandbox, Justin," she said in a choked voice. Justin walked over to the sandbox and climbed in, all the while keeping one eye on his mother.

"Please talk to your husband," Katie begged softly.

Anne shook her head and covered her face with her hands. Katie watched her sit that way for several long minutes. *She's not going to do it,* Katie worried. *She doesn't believe me!*

Katie glanced over at Scott sitting in the sandbox with the two kids. He shrugged his shoulders as if to say, *You did your best.* Then they both noticed Justin walking toward his mother. Scott turned him around so he faced away from Anne. "Let's make a castle, okay, big boy?" he asked as he handed Justin a shovel.

Katie turned back to Anne, who had not

moved. Her hands still covered her eyes.

"Anne," Katie tried again, "you've got to talk to your husband. Maybe he just doesn't realize how strong. . . ."

Then Anne looked up. "Greg has never hit Justin," she said quietly. "I did it."

Katie gasped.

"I just wanted to be a good mother!" Anne said. She started trembling so hard she could hardly talk. "I just wanted Justin to behave. I . . . I wanted Greg to be proud of him. And of me."

Katie sat close to Anne and put her arm around her. She couldn't believe Anne was the one who hit Justin. "But Justin told me his daddy spanks him."

Anne shook her head. "I told him his father *would* spank him, so Justin would do what I said. Greg never hit him at all. Or shook him," she whispered and closed her eyes. Then Anne stared at Laura, who had gone back to dragging her fingers through the sand and making chirping noises. "I didn't think I was really hurting him," she said softly.

Katie noticed Justin sitting in the sand, watching his mother closely. Scott must have seen him, too, because he called, "Hey, kids! Let's go swing!" Laura stood up and jabbered at him, while waving her arms. Justin looked at his mother uncertainly.

"Go ahead, honey," she told him in a strained voice. "I'll be over in a minute."

Anne and Katie watched Scott lead the kids over to the swings. "Oh, I didn't want to hit Justin," Anne insisted, "but it seemed like the only way I could get him to behave."

Katie just listened.

Anne shook her head and continued. "My mother used to hit us kids all the time. I guess I thought that was what all mothers did." She stared at her hands in her lap. "One time, though, I remember I went to school with a black eye. It was in third grade. I told everyone I fell off my bike."

Katie thought of what Mrs. Musgrove had said about raising kids the way your parents raised you.

Anne shook her head. "Justin seems to do things on purpose to make me mad. Do you know what he did last weekend, while I was trying to toilet train him?"

Katie shook her head.

"After he wet his pants, he'd hide them in a closet or under a bed. By the time I found them, everything stunk. Greg even found one pair. Justin just made me so angry, I shook him!" She looked away. "I finally gave up on the toilet training," she said. Katie could hardly hear her. "I guess he'll wear diapers forever."

"Maybe when he's a little older, he'll be ready for toilet training," Katie suggested.

Anne sighed. "Probably, but sometimes I think I'll be a hundred years old before that happens. This isn't how I imagined being a mother would be." Anne covered her face with her hands again.

When Anne looked up, her eyes were wet and red-rimmed. "Do you think . . . do you think Justin is brain-damaged, too?" she asked in a choked voice. "Is he going to be like that little girl?"

"I don't know," Katie said.

"That caseworker said she would come and check on Justin every week. She said . . . she said. . . ." Anne started to sob. Katie hugged her. *So Mrs. Musgrove had been there already,* she realized.

"She said if she saw more bruises, she'd take Justin away! Katie, he's my baby! She can't take him from me!" Katie held Anne while she cried.

Finally Anne raised her head. Her eyes were smudged with mascara. "The caseworker said she had to talk to Greg. She said this was his problem, too, that we both needed to go to parenting classes. She said we need to talk to other parents and learn more about kids Justin's age, so we'll know what's normal."

Katie just nodded. *Then maybe Justin won't have so many rules to follow,* she thought.

"But how can I tell Greg about all of this, Katie?"

"Maybe Mrs. Musgrove can help explain," Katie suggested. *Oops,* Katie thought. *If there was ever any doubt in Anne's mind that I told on her, she knows for sure now.*

Anne looked straight into Katie's eyes. "I know you already talked to her. I was furious about it."

Katie stared at her sneakers.

"But after seeing that little girl . . . and hearing about how she was hurt," Anne pressed her lips together to keep from crying again. "I didn't know that could happen. I could never live with myself if I hurt Justin like that." She shook her head. "I'm glad you talked with her, Katie."

Katie could not stop her tears. She almost didn't hear what Anne said next.

"Would you watch Justin while we go to the parenting classes?" Anne asked. "I do trust you." She tried to smile. "I think you must love Justin almost as much as I do."

Katie started to answer, but no words came out. Finally she just nodded. This time, Anne hugged her, and the tears fell down Katie's cheeks.

As Scott and Katie walked back to his house with Laura, Katie told him everything Anne had said.

"It sounds like Anne's really planning to go to the parenting classes," Scott said. "That's terrific! I bet Mr. Stuart will go, too, after Mrs. Musgrove talks to him."

"Even if Anne goes by herself at first," Katie added, "I think she'll start making changes. I bet she moves that last glass deer someplace high, where Justin can't reach it. That will sure make baby-sitting easier!"

Then Katie stopped walking. *Anne wants me to baby-sit again,* she realized. *I might make enough money for that dress! Maybe I can go to the Spring Dance after all!* She turned to Scott with red-rimmed eyes and a big smile on her face.

Fourteen

"I still think we should have gone to a movie," Scott said with a frown. He pulled at his stiff white collar.

"Scott!" Katie protested with a smile. "This dress wouldn't even fit into one of those seats!" She twirled around and her full white skirt billowed against his tuxedoed legs.

They could see Liz and Kenny dancing under the revolving light. After Liz had told Mike and Kenny about her predicament, Kenny had actually talked Mike into asking someone else to the dance. Now, Katie and Scott both grinned as they watched Mike tap on Kenny's shoulder in order to cut in.

Scott offered Katie a glass of punch. "How did baby-sitting go last night?" he asked.

Katie had watched Justin Friday night while his parents went to a big office party.

"Well, Anne was still in her bathrobe when I

got there," Katie said. "Justin had knocked an open bottle of shampoo into the bathtub just as she was running water to take a bath. Bubbles were foaming over the top and running down the outside!"

"I'm not sure I want to hear the end of this story," Scott said, with a serious look on his face.

Katie shook her head. "Things have really changed with the Stuarts! When I came in, Anne was hunting through the kitchen cabinets for her camera."

"Her camera?" Scott repeated.

Katie nodded. "She said she wanted to take pictures of the bathroom for a couple who just joined their parenting class. The other couple thinks their daughter is the only messy kid in the world. Anne said she wanted to show them that Justin gets the award for that!"

"Wow! A month of parenting classes has really made a difference!" Scott said.

Katie grinned. "I can't wait to see the picture. There were bubbles everywhere, and Justin, that little stinker, was giggling his head off!"

The band started to play a slow song. Scott took Katie's hand, and they walked out onto the dance floor.

"Anne looked so beautiful when she left,"

Katie said. "She was almost as excited about the party as I was about coming here tonight," she added shyly.

"I guess I'm glad we made it after all, Katie. But I don't know why having this dress was so important," Scott said.

"Well, because . . . because I wanted you to see what I look like dressed up," Katie mumbled.

Scott smiled at her. "After all the time we've spent studying together, I already know what you look like."

True, Katie told herself. *True.*

Then Scott pulled her a little closer. "Anyway, Katie—I know what's important to you . . . like a small child who needs help. I think you're beautiful." He tipped her face up. "And you didn't need this dress to prove that, Katie Weber."

Child Abuse—Some Facts

- Some common physical signs of abuse:
  - —bruises of varying ages
  - —burns, especially with odd patterns
  - —cuts and scrapes
  - —missing or loosened teeth
  - —bone injuries, especially in multiple or odd places
  - —head injuries
- Child abuse can occur in any type of family, rich or poor.
- Children who are abused still show love for the abusive parent and often protect him or her by not telling what is happening.
- Children who are abused often have high expectations placed on them.
- Anyone, including children, can report child abuse. Anyone who reports is protected by law and can remain anonymous.
- Child abuse *can* be treated and prevented.

The following are places you can write to or call for further information about child abuse:

THE NATIONAL COMMITTEE FOR PREVENTION
OF CHILD ABUSE
332 South Michigan
Suite 950
Chicago, Illinois 60604

CHILDHELP U.S.A.
The National Child Abuse Hotline
(A 24-hour hotline for crisis counseling and information
and referrals for child abuse)
1-800-4 A CHILD
(1-800-422-4453)

THE C. HENRY KEMPE NATIONAL CENTER FOR
THE PREVENTION AND TREATMENT OF CHILD
ABUSE AND NEGLECT
1205 Oneida
Denver, Colorado 80220

KIDSRIGHTS
(A clearinghouse of material about children
and their rights)
To obtain a free catalog:
3700 Progress Boulevard
Mount Dora, Florida 32757

You can also contact the Children's Protection Services located in your county of residence or your local children's hospital.

About the Author

LINDA BARR is a free-lance writer who also
volunteers as a puppeteer for Kids on the
Block, a program sponsored by The League
Against Child Abuse. Kids on the Block
teaches elementary schoolchildren about child
abuse and encourages them to ask for help if
they're being abused.

Linda hopes that readers of *I Won't Let
Them Hurt You* will become more aware of the
nature and prevention of child abuse and
speak up for children like Justin.

The author lives in Columbus, Ohio with her
husband, Tom, and their two children, Danny
and Colleen.